The Black Brothers

First published in German under the title *Die Schwarzen Brüder* in 1940
(Volume 1) and 1941 (Volume 2) by Verlag H.R. Sauerländer & Co. Aarau;
written by Kurt Kläber (alias Kurt Held) with Lisa Tetzner
and published under the name Lisa Tetzner.
Original copyright © 1941 by Sauerländer AG, CH-5001 Aarau.
Printed in China
All rights reserved
First American edition

Library of Congress Cataloging-in-Publication Data

Tetzner, Lisa, 1894-1963.
[Schwarzen Brüder. English]
The Black brothers: a novel in pictures / Lisa Tetzner;
pictures by Hannes Binder ; translated by Peter F. Neumeyer.
p. cm.
ISBN 1-932425-04-7 (alk. paper)
I. Binder, Hannes, 1947-   II. Neumeyer, Peter F., 1929-   II. Title.
PT2642.E84S3913 2004
833'.912-dc22   2004043238

The Black Brothers

A NOVEL IN PICTURES

Lisa Tetzner

PICTURES BY
Hannes Binder

TRANSLATED BY
Peter F. Neumeyer

FRONT STREET
Asheville, North Carolina

One morning in the late summer of 1838, a man walked down the Verzasca Valley. He moved quickly, seeming to have no time to notice the cliffs or even the trout that were leaping in the river. He looked straight ahead, furious that the town of Sonogno hadn't yet come into view.

There—finally he saw the first houses. Now that he knew he was near the village, he sat down by the side of the road. His gaze wandered up the steep precipices. There's no way to make a living here, he thought to himself. They've just got to give away their boys.

Giorgio had already been at work with his mother for hours. They were poor folk who fetched feed and hay from the steepest mountain slopes. The climb itself was difficult, and this high up the mountain they had to tie themselves to ropes in order to do the work.

Half the meadow had already been mowed. Giorgio kept pushing the cut hay farther up. How far away was his mother?

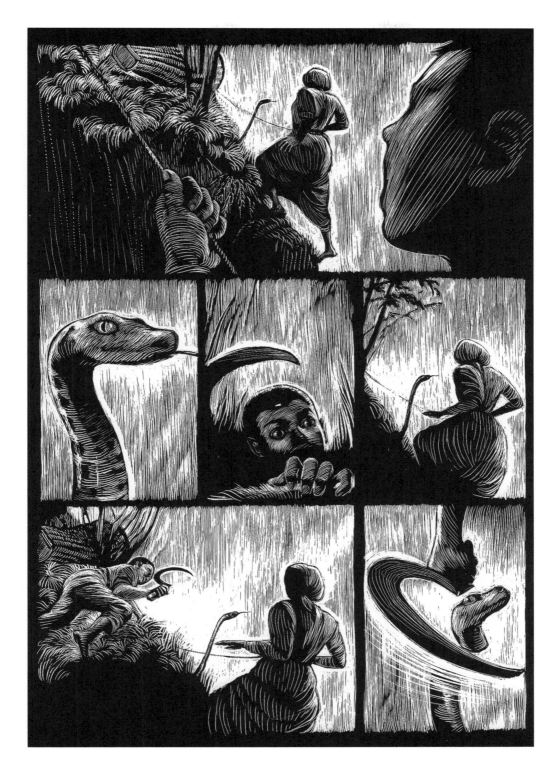

All over the ground there were vipers, but Giorgio and his mother didn't worry about such inconveniences. You just had to be quicker than the vipers.

For another hour, mother and son continued to work with their sickles. Then they piled up the grass, divided it into two baskets, and climbed down, slowly—just as they had come up. By then the man had arrived at the village.

In the evening, when Father came into the kitchen, he asked for strawberries. But Giorgio had forgotten to gather them in the forest.

"Twelve?" the father muttered. "You're twelve years old, and useless."

Silently they all spooned up their buckwheat porridge. Mother and Nonna helped the twins. And when they had finished, only Father got a piece of cheese.

Suddenly someone called out from the stable, "Roberto? Excuse …"
The maid from the inn entered. "There's somebody asking for you."
"Who?"
"Go look for yourself. He's got a scar on his face."
The father stood up. "I'll have to go see."

Roberto approached the man. "You want to speak to me?"

The man pushed a chair and a glass of wine toward him. "Drink first."

The two drank, looking at each other in silence. Giorgio's father didn't like the man. He stared ahead in a hard and evil way. And then, too, he had that wicked scar.

Father wanted to ask the man where he got it, but before he had a chance, the scarred one asked, "You've got a son?"

"Yes." Giorgio's father took a swallow of wine.

"He's thirteen?"

"He's going to be thirteen."

"I'm looking for boys like that."

"Well." Roberto took another swallow.

"I'll take them to Milan for a half year," the man continued. "I'll put them to work there. And for the father, thirty franks in payment for his son."

"I'm not going to sell my son for a *thousand* franks."

The man said merely, "Oh!"

"No," Roberto said, even louder this time. "So long as we have anything to eat and anything to drink, I'd sell the shirt off my back rather than my boy."

The man with the scar looked at him knowingly. "There's been many a one who has said that to me. And then suddenly there's no more wine; there's no more bread."

"So far, we've got enough of both," Roberto answered gruffly.

"I believe you," the man said soothingly. "I'll be back next year."

Roberto stood up. "Fine," he said, blinking at the man. "At that time we can talk again."

"You can depend on it." The man's face tightened in an odd way. "When I come back, you'll be happy to give me your boy to take to Milan."

"Happy, never," Roberto said. He pushed the empty glass aside and left.

The family was still sitting by the hearth when the father returned.

"What happened?" Mother asked.

"There really was a man with a scar who wanted to talk to me."

"And what did he want?"

"He buys children."

"Children!" the mother and grandmother exclaimed. And Giorgio, who came in with his father, looked up, frightened.

"The man wants to give me thirty franks." Father pointed to Giorgio. "For him there, if I let him take him to Milan for one winter."

"Thirty franks?" the mother repeated. "What would Giorgio do there?"

"Work," said the father.

"And what did you say to him?" The mother looked at him questioningly.

The father squinted. "Thirty franks isn't enough for such a big boy. He's really worth sixty to me."

"Oh, you black crow of a father!" the grandmother screamed, throwing a piece of wood at him.

"You don't think that was enough money?" The father looked at her and laughed. "And after all, next year he'll come back again."

"Why?"

"He says I'll gladly give him the boy for thirty franks then."

"That devil!" the mother exclaimed.

The father laughed again. "You're right. That's just what he looked like."

The next morning Giorgio rose early. At the path out of the village, he waited to intercept the man with the scar, but when he came Giorgio let him pass.

Giorgio was full of questions. But his mother didn't want to talk about it.

And his grandmother even less.

The father wanted to forget what the man had said.

"I'll be coming back next year."

The sentence was etched in their minds.

Then, whenever bad luck struck, they recalled that sentence.

And this year a great deal of bad luck came their way.

An icy winter was followed by a dry spring, and summer brought only drought.

Every day there was less grass, and for a long time the animals were reduced to eating foliage.

One afternoon Mother had climbed up a steep incline to cut twigs.

Since she had not returned by dark, Giorgio went out to look for her.

He found her lying unconscious. Her foot appeared to be broken. What now? How would they ever be able to pay for a doctor?

Sitting in the tavern two days later, the man with the scar already knew what had happened.

"Your time's up. This year you need me. I'll give you twenty franks."

"Damned cutthroat …"

"Five franks subtracted for each curse."

"Roberto," the innkeeper reminded the father. "Think of your wife."

Giorgio's father took a step toward the door. "When does he have to leave?"

"He has to be in Locarno the day after tomorrow. He should report at the Pan Perdu. That's the inn down by the lake. We'll go by fishing boat directly to Milan. And just remember one thing: It's the innkeeper who pays you. But only after he receives word that your son is in Locarno."

In the night the rain began. When Giorgio was wakened by Nonna, he could already see hundreds of little waterfalls tumbling down the slopes. He heard the roaring of the Verzasca higher up the ravine.

His mother lay feverish in her bed, groaning with every motion. "You're not going to Locarno in this weather, are you?"

"I am," Giorgio replied, knowing full well that the man with the scar expected him that evening in the Pan Perdu. "Goodbye, Mother, rest quietly now. Tomorrow the doctor will be here for sure, and then all your pain will be taken care of."

Nonna had packed up polenta sandwiches, a bit of goat cheese, a little bread, and some grapes for the boy.

"Farewell," she said, and kissed Giorgio on his forehead.

"Farewell." He shook hands with her, shouldered his bag, and went to the stable.

His father was standing in the rain and laughing. Giorgio could tell from how his shoulders shook.

"I'm leaving, Father."

Suddenly his father's face grew sad and the laughter vanished. With all that happiness about the rain, Roberto had almost forgotten that his son would be leaving today.

"Are you angry with me, Giorgio?"

"No, Father. Just as long as you get the money for Mother. Next year I'd have to go into some line of work anyhow."

"I knew it, Giorgio—thirteen and you're already very brave. And it's only for a few months, after all."

Giorgio felt sick. Should he tell his father what Anita had told him? She had heard that many chimneysweep boys actually died in that work.

"Have you got all your things in order?" his father asked.

"In the afternoon Anita is coming to fetch my woodpecker, the titmice, and my owl. The bunny should go to the twins."

"Farewell." They shook hands. "Farewell."

Giorgio slipped into the church one last time. He wanted to ring in the day, just as he had done every other day. A couple of women were already in the first pew, uttering prayers of thanksgiving for the rain.

Giorgio rang the bells. Once again he sent his greetings up to the owls in the steeple. He left the church through the back exit. And now for the last time he was supposed to whistle in front of Anita's house. Instead he made a wide detour. She would find out soon enough that he had left for Milan.

Then he saw her. She was standing precisely on the spot where, a year ago, Giorgio had been on the lookout for the man with the scar. She walked toward him.

"Are you going to leave? You promised me that you'd stay."

He shook his head. "I didn't promise you anything."

"Yes, you did."

"But—Father needs the money for Mother. I have to go get the doctor in Locarno."

"Oh," said Anita, moving a step closer. "I'm afraid for you."

He tried to laugh. "I'm staying for just six months. Next year at this time I'll be here again—with you."

"If only that turns out to be true."

Even though the rain came down and water ran in rivulets down his head and neck and body, Giorgio went with great speed. Sometimes he had to wade through raging streams, in water up to his knees.

It was market day in Locarno, and in all the valleys here and in the valleys on the other side, men and women were on the move.

Giorgio told the farmers he overtook that he was going to the doctor for his mother.

"Oh, so then you're Roberto's son. Not so fast, not so fast. It's always better to have company when you walk. Would you stay next to my animal? It calms him down to have somebody close by when we cross streams."

The older man led a donkey laden with bales of cloth: white and dark linen, as well as a few colored bales. The other man carried a leather pouch containing two dozen eggs and a couple of chunks of butter.

The sun shone through weakly, but the clouds still hung low in the valleys, and the swollen streams roared down the steep precipices.

In Brione the two farmers sought shelter, inviting Giorgio to join them. He thanked them but said he was in a hurry, and then he proceeded alone.

But right after Giorgio had passed the village, he had to wait anyway. A second stream plunged from an adjacent valley down into the Verzasca. It carried with it wood, branches, tree limbs, and rubble, pouring them into the river with such violence that the opposite shore was flooded. Nobody could proceed.

A couple of farm wives shouted angrily, "What are we supposed to do? We must get to Locarno. We've got to sell the last things we can get rid of there, and now we're not even going to get to the market."

"Somebody has to go back to Brione," said another woman. "We must get the men."

But just then the two farmers came back, and with them, on horseback, the priest from Brione, and two young men who were driving their sheep and goats to Locarno.

Seeing the flooded embankment, the priest announced, "I'll turn back and wait till help comes."

The young men wanted to take their herds by the high path. Giorgio joined them, going up the steep mountainside. An hour later they were descending back down into the Verzasca Valley.

Here the land spread out, broad and fruitful. There were still puddles in the fields of corn and wheat, and beside the small path broad torrents of water were rushing.

Later, in Lavertezzo, they came upon still more people headed for the market. A tinker and his apprentice had come along and were on their way over the double-arch bridge. Joining them also were a straw weaver carrying his work basket on his back and a couple of farmers hoping to sell their honey.

After St. Bartolomeo the path became narrower. At one point it was so steep that Giorgio was frightened. He crawled more than he walked, grasping the boulders with his hands. Down below tumbled the torrents of the Verzasca. Between the boulders it was often dark. Finally, Giorgio emerged again into the blazing sun.

Locarno

Minusio

Lago Maggiore

Just before Vogorno, the men felled a large chestnut tree. Grabbing for the limbs, they groped their way across this emergency bridge. And then there were still more tributary streams to get around. Finally, they struggled up the mountain on goat paths, and then down again on icy crevasses, down to the Verzasca Valley.
A one-hour detour. And then for the first time Giorgio saw the lake, Lago Maggiore, which Father and Grandmother—Nonna—had talked about.

Giorgio now walked alone; he strode forth. The plain of Locarno lay ahead of him. And soon he was hungry. But his food was soggy. When he tossed the doughy mush into a pond, a trout rose.

Lavertezio

Vogorno

Gordola

Tenero

When he came up for air, Giorgio heard high-spirited laughter. A youngster was standing there, and although his clothes were in tatters, he had a princely air about him.

"What are you laughing at? Come on into the water and help me catch trout."

Giorgio showed the boy his food bag, demonstrating how he was able to drive fish into it. Then, having found only wet wood, the other boy went to a nearby stable to gather hay. Quickly they made a fire.

"What's your name, anyway?"

"Alfredo."

"I'm Giorgio. Where do you come from?"

"From Valle Mesocco."

"Is that far away?"

"Just a couple of hours."

Short questions, evasive answers. Giorgio looked into Alfredo's eyes.

Suddenly a thought struck. "Are you going to Milan?"

Alfredo looked up, astonished. "How do you know?"

"Because … because I have to go to Milan myself."

"You! I thought you were from the village, here."

Giorgio explained about his mother, about the money for the doctor. "And what about you?"

Alfredo muttered something and then let slip, "There's a secret involved."

"A secret?" Now Giorgio's curiosity was aroused. But then Alfredo unpacked some bread.

Later he wanted them to swear allegiance to each other. "Like the knights in my book."

"You know how to read!" Giorgio's mouth dropped open.

"I know how to write, too."

Giorgio shook his head. "And you're going to Milan as a chimneysweep?"

"I didn't say that. There's a secret. Come on, or we won't make it to Locarno."

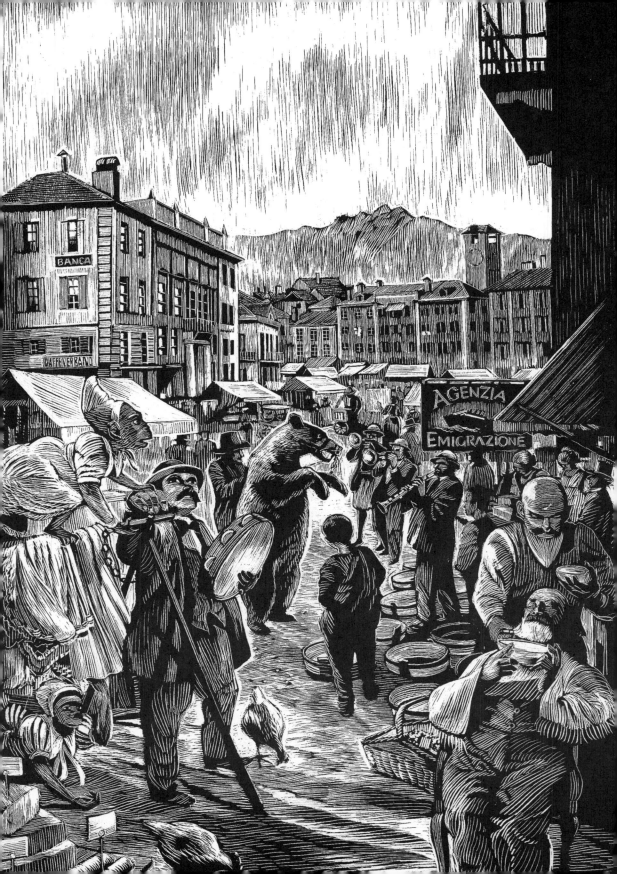

Giorgio could not get over his amazement. He had never seen a city before. With Alfredo's help he asked how to get to the doctor's house. A plaster façade, a brass door knocker—Giorgio had never seen such elegance. A maid opened the door and promised that the doctor would go see the mother—and he'd go soon, she said, for he had to travel in that direction anyway. Giorgio thanked her, and then the two boys slipped back into the tumult of the weekly market.

Music, animals, and unfamiliar people looking at the merchandise, talking about the prices. The boys stood still, but then they were again pressed forward by the crowd. Alfredo was the one who knew his way around. He explained many things. And the boys forgot all about the time.

A girl stood next to a man with a hurdy-gurdy. She sang about a great fire, and with a stick she pointed to a picture. Was that a picture of Milan?

Then somebody pushed through the crowd of listeners. Giorgio was frightened.

"Hey, you. Who is that other one?"

Giorgio pointed to Alfredo.

"Are you a chimneysweep?"

"Yes, I am," Alfredo said, nodding. "I'm from Valle Mesocco. A man from Como recruited me. I was supposed to be here today."

"Then come with me, you rascals. I've been looking all over for you."

They followed him behind the tents to where the farmers' horses and donkeys were kept. They stumbled along a narrow lane down to the lake.

At first, the boys saw only a tall house and a thick wall. Then the gate opened, and a dark man with piercing eyes waved them in.

They stood in the ruins of a courtyard. The dark one pushed the boys toward a shed.

"I'm hungry," Alfredo protested, pulling away.

"I'm not feeding you," the dark one laughed. "I'm only taking you across."

He yanked open the door of the hut and shoved the boys in.

"Ouch!" someone cried out. Giorgio fell over a pair of legs.

"Is somebody there?" he asked.

"Somebody?" a voice repeated. "At least two dozen of us."

From the direction of the lake, light still penetrated. Giorgio could now see that the large shed was full of boys.

"Lie down," the voice said again. "And don't make a racket. We've been walking all day, and we're tired."

"We are too," Giorgio and Alfredo replied.

"All the better. Then you'll be asleep soon." He pushed straw toward the two, and then rolled over to face the other way.

"Good night, Giorgio." Alfredo lay next to him.

All you could hear was the snoring of the sleepers and the soft, regular lapping of the water.

Soon Giorgio awoke. Outside, men were cursing. They were talking about two chimneysweeps who froze to death in Milan last winter. There was also talk of the local authorities and the customs officers.

"They ought to be happy. We're providing money for the poor," one of the men muttered.

"I've always paid their fathers," another shouted. "Everything according to the law! There's nothing here that's illegal. Many of these kids are volunteers anyway."

Giorgio didn't understand what this talk was about.

Suddenly the shack door was ripped open: "Out. Get up. We're leaving!"

The slow ones were pushed along. *"Avanti!* Get on the boat."

"I'm afraid. I'm scared of water," a scrawny boy whimpered.

"Me too," said another. "I'm scared. I've never been …"

"Shut your traps!" screamed the man with the scar. He grabbed one of the boys by his shirt and dragged him into the boat.

"Did you count them?" the man with the scar asked. He was the last to jump into the boat.

"There's twenty-one by my count," said the boatman.

"Then we're on target. I'm number twenty-two."

"That's a lot for this worn-out boat," the boatman muttered, taking his oars.

"Either of you know how to row?" asked the man with the scar, pointing to two of the boys.

"Me," announced Alfredo. The other one also knew how.

"Good." The man with the scar handed them the oars. "I'm taking the rudder."

When Giorgio came to the surface, he saw only hands and arms. The boys' screams were drowned out in the roaring of the water. The next waves broke over everything. When Giorgio surfaced again, the boat had disappeared. He grasped a plank and pulled his body up on it. Now he was able to look around.

"Alfredo!"

At first the two boys hung desperately on to the plank. But after a short time they figured out what they had to do. They were too exhausted to talk. A puff of wind blew the fog aside.

"Look!" gasped Giorgio. "The shore. No, the other side is closer. Hang on. I'll push."

"Over there! Someone else is swimming—one of the men."

For a long time the man with the scar lay as though he were dead. Then his eyes slowly opened. "You? Why did you save me?" He snorted. "You know what I would have done in your place? I'd have let Antonio Luini drown, and then I'd have gotten myself home as fast as I could."

Giorgio jumped up. "But that's not something we could do."

"No, it's too late. I paid for you and I'd soon track you to your homes again."

"I don't have a home," Alfredo burst out.

Giorgio looked over at him. Alfredo turned away, embarrassed.

"You're going to go to the village now. Tell them what happened, but don't say that you rescued me. They know me hereabouts, and for rescuing me they'd toss you back into the water. Get going now; I'll wait for you."

Cannobio was the name of the place. The storm had driven them far to the south. The first person they met was a customs official. He noted their wet clothing.

"What's the story with you?"

Giorgio told him. The customs official got the picture right away.

"Was that Antonio with you too? Hasn't the devil fetched him yet?"

"I think," said Alfredo, "that we're the only two who survived. The rest have probably drowned."

The customs man ran off to the church. The bells began to ring, and everywhere people streamed out of their houses. The official shouted something, and the people ran to the lake.

The boys sneaked off, unseen.

When the village lay far behind them, they felt free again.

Suddenly, there in front of them, was the man with the scar. He had been waiting in a field of corn. "That took you a while. But you made it all right."

Without turning around he began to walk.

"Did you find out whether they managed to rescue anyone else?"

The boys shook their heads and remained silent.

"It's a lost cause. The boat went down an hour ago. Now, hop to it! We've got to get as far as Pallanza."

"Hungry?" The man turned around, looking scornful. Nonetheless, in the next town he bought sausage and bread. A bit later they sat down near the water. The man broke the bread into three pieces. The sausage, however, he kept for himself.

Soon he got the boys up and going again.

Several oxcarts rolled toward them. The farmers, on the way to their fields, waved at them. But the man with the scar only looked away. He wasn't at all happy that anyone should see them, and certainly he didn't return the greetings.

"I can't go on," Giorgio panted.

"Me neither," Alfredo complained.

The man with the scar scolded, but all the same, he headed in the direction of the lake, where he crawled into the bushes. Hardly had he lain down than he was snoring. Alfredo, too, went to sleep immediately. Giorgio had never slept outdoors before. Frogs croaked, crickets chirped. Everything seemed familiar to him, and new at the same time. Then he heard the *kiwi, kiwi* of a small owl. Back in Sonogno—he was just there two days ago!—was Anita now looking after his animals? Had the doctor already visited his mother? And then Giorgio heard screams, saw again the faces of the drowning boys, heard the wind, and now, nothing but waves. Black.

The next morning, as they went along the back lanes of Stresa, the bells chimed. Silently people came toward them on their way to church. For a moment the man left the boys alone, but then he pushed them on again. A young man with horse and wagon caught up with them, and the man with the scar asked whether they could have a ride.

"Hop up," said the young man, gesturing toward the back with his whip.

After a while he asked where they had come from.

"From Locarno," answered the man with the scar.

"On foot?"

The scarred one nodded.

"Then you're in luck," the young man babbled on. "Yesterday twenty boys and two men came from Locarno on a boat. Even though there was a storm. At Cannobio the boat sank. Except for two of the boys, they're all thought to have drowned. They're looking for them now. If you weren't right here with me, sir, I'd say it was you."

"I heard about that in Stresa," the man with the scar replied. "They were just saying a mass for them—yes, poor boys, poor men."

47

"Well, I don't care about the men. These slave-traders don't deserve any better. But the children …"

The man with the scar turned silent. It seemed all right with him that, a little later, the wagon driver had to go off in another direction.

The night they spent in a little grove seemed short. Mosquitoes plagued the sleepers and made them get under way while it was still dark. The fields became larger, the rivers broader.

Whenever the three came across a traveler, the man didn't let the boys out of his sight. And when he bought bread and sausages, he gave them only bread.

Giorgio and Alfredo were exhausted. They were tired of being on their feet, of keeping their eyes open. They wanted only to lie down.

"Is it a long way to Milan still?"

"If you were as tall as I am, you could already see it."

A few steps more and the boys climbed up the embankment. But all they could see was a pale fog.

The man stood next to them. "You still don't see anything?"

The boys shook their heads.

"Over there, that tower. That's Santa Maria delle Grazie. And over on that side, see the many little steeples, and there's the dome."

The boys had no idea which little steeples he was talking about. They merely nodded.

Ever more houses bordered the country road, and everywhere there were people bustling about. Frequently there were houses on both sides of the road at the same time.

Once Giorgio heard children's voices. He looked across. Was it men and women who were playing? No, it was children. Giorgio had never seen children wearing such fancy clothes—children in adult clothing.

"Look at that house," Giorgio called out. "Look how high it is."

It was as tall as five houses on top of each other in Sonogno. Giorgio began to count the windows. "... twelve, thirteen, four—"

"Watch out!" screamed the man with the scar, yanking the boys aside as a heavy coach rattled past.

"Damn it!" the man scolded. "I haven't dragged you all the way to Milan just to have you fall under the first carriage!"

Now the boys began to be more careful. But they still kept stopping, even though the man was pushing and scolding them.

Every step showed them something they had never seen before. Benches on which you could sit down right there in the middle of the city. Little children in double file, pattering out of a church.

"Come on, come on!" the man with the scar was nagging once again. "Or am I going to have to force you to get moving?"

But again they were staring at a café. The tables extended all the way out to the street, and ladies and gentlemen were sitting at each one of them, the ladies dressed as brightly as parrots.

A column of Austrian soldiers was marching past when suddenly a troop of riders came galloping around the corner. And before the boys recovered from that scare, they found themselves standing in the cathedral square.

"Like a giant pastry."

"No," said Giorgio, "like the icicles which hang in the Verzasca gorge in winter."

"Okay, so a whole iceberg," the man with the scar muttered. "But now if you don't get moving, I'll let you have it."

He herded them along, away from the cathedral square into a broad street.

"Now, up there around the corner. There's the Golden Pot. That's where we've got to go."

As soon as the boys had been herded into the tavern, conversation stopped.

The customers stared at them. Then one exclaimed, "Is it really you? We've just now drunk to your death, Antonio."

They all began speaking at once. The newspapers had spread word of the accident. But there hadn't been a word about the man with the scar being rescued.

"Did the two boys rescue you?"

"And in spite of that, you drag them here? You ungrateful devil!"

For a long time the boys heard harsh words up there, in the room above the cellar.

The next morning, Giorgio and Alfredo scrubbed their faces. They were supposed to look fresh and healthy, for no sooner had the first chimneysweep boss arrived than the bargaining began.

"Is that all the boys you've got?" asked the master chimneysweep with the pale yellow face.

"Yes," said the innkeeper. "I've already said, the others drowned."

"And when are you going to get new ones?"

"You have to wait! We have to be careful, till … first the authorities have to look away, and then the newspapers have got to settle down."

"I like the one over there better." Another master chimneysweep crowded forward and pointed to Alfredo. "Let me see. Are you strong?" He grabbed for Alfredo's arms. "How much does he cost?"

"Eighty. I'm offering eighty," the first chimneysweep said.

"Eighty-two," replied the innkeeper.

"Eighty-two. I can get a goat for that!"

"Then go ahead and buy a goat and let her sweep your chimneys."

Other chimney masters came in. One had a little goatee. Another one was round as a ball, with a broad and friendly face.

"Oh, Battista. Hello, Emilio." The innkeeper shook hands with each.

"Well," said the one with the goatee, "at least you rescued two good ones. How much for that one?"

Short sentences, sparse words. The two masters were prepared to pay.

The fat one drew out a purse. His coins rang clear on the table. Goatee wanted to give the innkeeper four bills.

The yellow-faced one grabbed him: "Damn. I bid first."

"But only eighty. Now settle down or …"

"…or what?" hissed Yellow Face, and drew a knife.

"Forget it!" shouted the innkeeper. "Go on outside to kill yourselves."

Angry, the yellow-faced one turned away. He put the knife back, gave the innkeeper eighty-two lire, and pulled Alfredo outside.

Alfredo barely had time to look back. "Ciao, Giorgio."

Calmly the other master emptied the glass that the innkeeper had offered him. Then in friendly fashion he tapped Giorgio on the shoulder and went on ahead.

In daytime there was even more to see in the streets than there had been in the evening.

"Come on," said Master Rossi over and over again. "Come on. The city's not going to run away from you. What you don't see today, you can see tomorrow."

They proceeded out across the square and entered a church. Never had Giorgio dreamed that there existed such huge spaces. You could put all of Sonogno inside it! The master was already at the back exit. Again they stepped out into the open.

"We'll be there any minute. Now remember these streets. Pretty soon you'll have to find your way around by yourself."

They turned into an alley where people were filing, sawing, mending, and hammering. It smelled of tar and glue, of wood smoke and dye.

"Is that your new boy?" the cobbler called out.

Master Rossi nodded.

"Pale, he's looking. Mighty pale."

"Yes," ventured the tailor next door. "You're going to have to feed that one well or he'll keel over."

They laughed. The master waved and passed through a gate to the house in back.

"The poor little kid," a woman said. "How in the world can people send such little children to work in the city?"

The master climbed up the stairs.
Doors. Doors. Doors. Giorgio looked at
them.

"So," said the master, "here's where
we live."

He opened a door and stepped into a
corridor. Way in the back, Giorgio saw a
partition set at an angle. In front of that,
an open door—to the kitchen? There
was a smell of onions.

"You finally here?" asked a
screeching woman's voice.

"Yes," the master answered.

"Did you get a boy?"

"Yes." The master went into the
kitchen. Giorgio remained in the corridor.
He looked around.

"Well, where is he?" asked the voice.
"Boy! Come on in here."

The woman turned out to be just like her voice.

"Is he any good? How much did you pay for him?" Her voice rose higher still. "Go on, tell me. Or do I have to count the money myself?" She grabbed for the man's pocket.

"Lay off!"

"What do you mean, 'Lay off'? Tell me or I'll …"

"There were only two …"

"What do you mean, two? How much did you pay?"

The woman scolded, and the master remained silent.

Then, when she insisted that surely there were many parents who wanted to get rid of their boys, her husband replied, "You're not giving yours away. If I were to take Anselmo …"

"Anselmo!" she shouted. "My Anselmo! Oh you vulture! You miserable …"

At that point the door to a room opened. A boy looked out.

"Did you hear that? Your father wants to send you into the chimneys. What do you say to that?"

"No, I don't want any such thing," said Master Rossi. "I just said that because you … Oh, come on, let's drop it. I'm hungry."

"Ah, his highness is hungry! From doing what? From standing around?" the woman hissed. But then she ladled soup from the pot, and the three gulped it down eagerly.

When the master finally looked up, his glance fell on Giorgio, who was still standing there.

"Doesn't the boy get anything to eat?"

"No, first he's got to work. Maybe this evening."

In the end, though, the woman did put a plate in front of Giorgio. "There. Go on and eat."

Later she filled another plate and carried it out. Giorgio heard her now talking in a friendly voice, almost gently.

"Father!"

Master Rossi left Giorgio standing in the hallway and disappeared into a little room.

"Where are you going, Father?" Giorgio again heard a little girl's voice.

"We're both going off to work."

"Both of you? Do you have a new boy?"

"Yes."

"Then let him come in." Giorgio was already standing in the doorway.

"This is our daughter," said Master Rossi. "Her name is Angeletta. She's sick."

"Yes," the girl whispered. "For two years now I haven't been able to get up. The doctor won't let me. What's your name?"

"Yes, what *is* your name?" repeated the master, asking for the first time.

"Giorgio."

"You still here?" came a shrill voice from the kitchen.

"Yes, Mother," said the girl. "They've stayed a moment. I wanted to look at the new boy."

"Not much to see in him," snarled the woman. "Come on, get going now. The child is supposed to sleep after she eats."

"Well, I like him," said the girl.

"I don't," growled Anselmo, who had come in with his mother.

The master pushed Giorgio out the door.

Down in the yard there was a little shed. The master took out a ladder, rope, other tools, and a few brushes. Some of these he put in his sack; others he hung over Giorgio's shoulder.

"So, now—from here on, this is what you're going to carry."

It was hot in the streets, even though the sun shone on only half the houses. Behind the church, they turned into the broad street.

"Here. Via Manzoni—that's our territory."

The master walked ahead slowly, scanning the high façades.

"*Spazzacamino, spazzacamino!*—Chimneysweeps, chimneysweeps!—We're here to clean your chimneys!"

Giorgio was startled by the power of the master's voice.

"*Spazzacamino, spazzacamino!* Come on, boy, why aren't you shouting too? You think I want to shout myself hoarse all alone?"

"I … ah … I … You didn't say anything about shouting."

"Do I have to tell you everything first? Just do what I do."

So Giorgio began shouting too.

Soon they took turns.

"Over there, somebody is waving. Get up, quick!"

"Where?" Giorgio asked.

"Up there."

"How do we get up there?"

"Through the door, stupid!"

Broad stairs, pictures on the walls. Everywhere, carpets and polished furniture. The boy was amazed. He stopped, motionless.

"Get a move on."

Puzzled, Giorgio looked at the master.

"Come on, crawl in!"

"Into that hole?"

"Yes, into that hole."

"What am I supposed to do in there?"

"Close your eyes and get in there. There, stretch that arm. There's a piece of iron up there. Can you feel it? Pull yourself up on that. And keep going. Till you're up top."

"But what am I supposed to do?"

"When you feel chimney holes left and right, you push into them."

"How …? What am I to use for …?"

"Don't ask so many questions! With your hands. And let the soot fall."

Giorgio shut his eyes. He groped for the first iron, pulled himself up. Soot fell, pouring on top of him like a stream and trickling down his back.

The boy climbed even higher.

He felt the holes. He pushed into them, pulling out the soot, and climbing higher yet.

The chimney narrowed.

His eyes burned; they were full of soot. His nose was clogged.

Giorgio could breathe only through his mouth. He became dizzy.

Using his feet, he groped his way back.

"What! Back already?"
   "I can't take any more."
   "Well then, blow out. And then back up you go."

"*Spazzacamino, spazzacamino!*"
   Into the homes, up the chimney.
   Day after day. Week after week.
   "Black man! Black man!" Children ran, mocking, behind them.
   Giorgio shook his fist and was going to … "Let it go!" said the master.
"Don't look at them. *Spazzacamino, spazzacamino!*"

One day a baker lad came running. Even when he was still a good way off, he
was calling and waving Master Rossi and Giorgio to come into the back yard.

The oven was hot.

Giorgio could barely breathe.

He became frightened, but he absolutely had to climb …

The only way was upward.

Filled with despair, he climbed just like that time when …

Startled by an eagle (Giorgio recalled), a goat and her kid got into the ravine and plummeted down.

The kid was still alive and whimpered as it hung on to some scrub.

His father let Giorgio down the precipice on a rope. But when finally the boy reached the injured animal, the eagle, too, shot down to snatch up his prey.

Giorgio threw stones at him.

The eagle rose into the sky again. Now Giorgio could shoot the old rifle.

The kid was rescued, and the boy was celebrated as a hero. But the kid lived only a few days, and the goat stayed dead.

Was that the bad luck the man with the scar spoke of? He had said to the father that disaster comes quicker than you expect. And then he had said, "I shall return."

When Giorgio opened his eyes, he was lying on the floor of the baking room. Somebody had thrown water on him. Several people were staring at him; others were talking to the baker.

Master Rossi cleared his throat. He reached out his hand to Giorgio and helped him to his feet. Then he put the lighter of the sacks on Giorgio's back and went on ahead, out into the street.

"A good-for-nothing gets nothing," said Signora Rossi later in the kitchen, and her husband didn't contradict her.

Giorgio was locked in, as he had been every other night. Grinning, Anselmo had seen to that.

Exhausted, Giorgio tossed, unable to sleep.

Toward midnight, Giorgio heard Angeletta's door, and then her footsteps.

The first time the girl stood in front of his small partition, he was frightened.

Since then, their shared secret was Giorgio's consolation. It eased his homesickness and helped him forget the nightmares of soot and smoke.

Silently, Angeletta slid back the bolt and led the way into her room.

She retrieved a plate from beneath her bed.

"This is for you."

Polenta sandwiches and stuffed tomatoes. That was just what Anselmo had been eating for dinner, smacking his lips loudly in order to torment Giorgio.

"And you? Aren't you eating anything?"

"Just go ahead and take it. And then you've got to tell me. But quietly, so that Mother can't hear."

"Tell you what?"

"About yourself. Again, about your home. About how you lived in Ticino and about the animals."

Giorgio had told her these stories many times. That his father hadn't wanted to give him away. But then the harsh winter came. The first snow fell when the grapes were still on their vines. And then it got colder and colder. Mercilessly cold. Nobody recalled a time past when it had been this cold.

Nonna had told them that, long ago, even bears were seen—farther up the valley.

But Giorgio saw only foxes. Foxes in the daytime! Right in the middle of the town.

Wild birds too were looking for food there among all the people.

And the people themselves would huddle around the hearth, day and night.

"Like in a cave," said Angeletta.

She understood the misery Giorgio was telling her about.

But even so, she listened to his stories as though they were fairy tales, gripping stories of adventure.

And that cold winter was followed by a dry summer.

The crops withered before they bore seed.

Already in May the farmers had to drive the cattle up to the farthest meadows. Down in the valley everything was as though it had been burned. And soon it did burn, in fact. As the fire flared up the slopes, the cows had to be driven even farther—across dangerous paths that they would never have ventured on before.

Angeletta knew that in the past a cow had tumbled down, and that Giorgio's mother broke her foot. The boy had often told about his mother, and about Anita as well. But by this time Giorgio had fallen asleep, right in the middle of the story he was telling her.

After a while Angeletta awakened him.

Giorgio didn't mind moving back to his bed of straw.

The only thing that mattered at this moment was that Angeletta could fetch him back from there unnoticed.

The next day they were back on the streets. They quickly found a customer. But although Giorgio had by now been inside many fancy houses, he'd never seen one as elegant as this: bookcases in the hallway, heavy carpets everywhere, and then there was the man himself … a man who, here in his own home, was dressed as though for a celebration.

"I wanted to burn papers, documents, yesterday. But the chimney didn't draw. That's why I called you."

"At your service," said the master and knelt down in the fireplace. "There must be something stuck in the chimney. It's not that high, so I ought to see some light at least. Come on, Giorgio, up with you!"

Rapidly the boy climbed up until … there was something prickly. Wood? Straw?

Giorgio tugged at it, and quickly it slid past him, falling to the bottom.

The chimney was empty once again.

"A bird's nest!" the man exclaimed. "My feathered friends have been living with me and I didn't even know it. Or did I? Was that the blackbird that I occasionally heard singing? 'Fiu-fiu—fiu-fiu …'"

The man sat down at the piano. Nimbly he played the keys. Then he got up and sang in an unexpectedly fine voice.

Giorgio now heard the chirps of birds. He saw blackbirds, finches … the nest he had found in the church tower, the little owl he had caught in order to show it to Anita.

The chirping of the birds. Their soft feathers
and the little heart that beats so mightily.

The rushing of the Verzasca, the cool air,
when the heat above is so oppressive.
Giorgio liked to work among the vegetable plots.
Mother had got them started down below, in the ravine.

The very best berry patches of Sonogno were close by.
He had shown them only to Anita.
With her he shared all his secrets.

Down in the gulch, he had also observed the badger.
Never, ever, would he have betrayed the secret place if …
… if one morning Father hadn't observed great damage done to the corn.
Giorgio immediately recognized the tracks in the ground.
So he decided to take old rifle to the badger lodge.

The song of the blackbird.
Eating berries with Anita.
The song of the mountain finches.

The maid's voice interrupted Giorgio's reveries. "Have you not given him the money yet?"

Surprised, the man at the piano looked up and smiled at Giorgio.

"That will be one lira, if you please," said Master Rossi

Not long after that, it happened again that Giorgio almost suffocated in a chimney. When they got back out to the street, he had to vomit.

"I can't go on." He sat at the edge of the curb.

"We can't go back home this early."

"I really can't anymore."

"Well, come along then. We'll drink a schnapps."

The master went ahead, into the tavern.

If only he'd drive off the boys who were taunting Giorgio.

Children running behind the chimneysweeps were a normal part of the scene, like rust in the chimney. Giorgio was used to the teasing and hardly turned around anymore to face the children. But there were days when the soot burned in his eyes and the taunting of the boys hurt. Worst of all was the gang that hung around the boy with the pockmark scars. He would bully and torment worse than all the others because, long ago, he learned that the master would call Giorgio to him whenever the boy wanted to fight back. Now the gang laughed more wildly than before.

But Rossi just marched ahead.

He was thinking only of his schnapps.

"There." The master pushed a glass toward him. Giorgio sniffed it and hesitated.

"Close your eyes, boy, and gulp it down."

Giorgio shuddered. Still, even though the schnapps burned in his throat like hot pepper, it made him feel better. Obviously, the master liked it. He continued to drink and laugh and gossip with his friends.

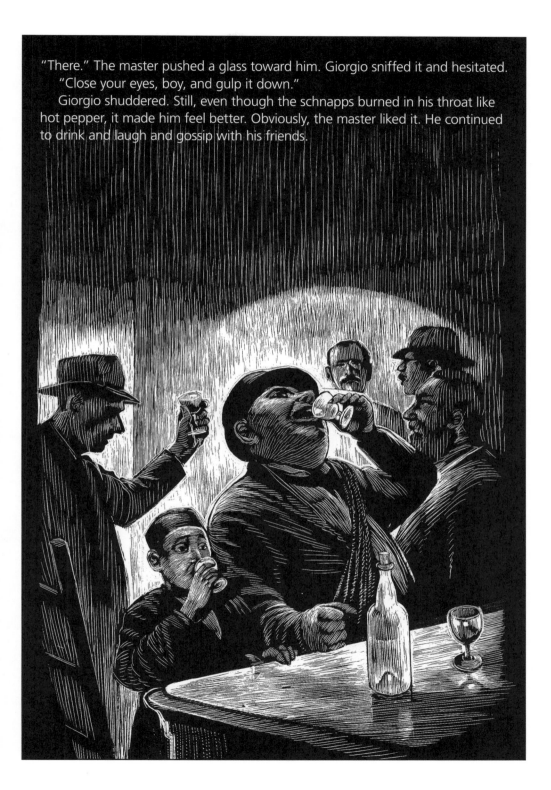

It was getting dark when the two stepped back outside. Now it was Giorgio's turn to keep the master going. For another half hour the two walked up and down the streets, looking for chimneys to sweep. But however loudly they called, nobody wanted their services now.

On the other hand, the pockmarked one was still there with his gang. Giorgio kept turning around to challenge them.

Finally the master said, "It would be best for us to go home now."

As Giorgio steered him through the streets, even the other tradesmen were mocking them.

"Like master, like apprentice!"

"We used to have pity for the young one; now he's pale from drinking."

Giorgio already sensed what awaited them at the top of the stairway.

He took the tools to the shed, washed up, and went upstairs.

Next morning, everything was even worse. The master discovered that his coin purse was missing from his jacket pocket. Two lire were in it.

"You've drunk those away," his wife taunted. But it was Giorgio whom she grabbed and beat and searched.

"He hid the purse long ago," Anselmo called out from the kitchen. "I saw him when he was fussing around the closet."

"No, I'm not a thief. I'm not!"

"If not you, who then?" Signora Rossi beat him some more and shouted at her husband.

Finally the master pulled the boy away. "It's time; we have to go."

"What's the matter? You going to protect him? You just wait—we're going to find that money."

"Yes," Anselmo shouted. "We're going to search his lair."

They can search all they want to, Giorgio thought with relief.

That was still what he thought even when Signora Rossi stood in front of the house at noon.

"Here comes the thief," she called out to the neighbors. She held the coin purse under her husband's nose. "Here! This was hidden in his nest. Now you know what sort of creature you brought into our house. A rascal, that's what he is!"

She beat Giorgio, and the people standing about egged her on. Master Rossi, too, was now convinced of Giorgio's guilt. But he didn't want to pursue the matter out in the street. He grabbed the boy by the ear and pulled him after himself up into the lodging.

"You've not only stolen from me, you've lied to me as well."

"No, by everything that's holy to me, it really wasn't me."

"Liar! Thief!" Signora Rossi beat on Giorgio with her wooden shoe until he bled.

"Mama, what are you doing?" Angeletta stood in the doorway of her room. "Stop beating him. I won't lie down until you—"

"But he's a thief. He stole money from your father."

"Even so, you can't beat him. Promise me."

"Fine," said Master Rossi. "He'll be locked up until he confesses."

"Let me do it," said Anselmo, shoving Giorgio into the closet.

Giorgio was hurting all over his whole body, but most painful to bear were the false accusations. If Angeletta had not intervened, they'd have beaten him to death. Even the master didn't trust him anymore. And suddenly he was gone. Where?

When Signora Rossi or Anselmo scolded him, Giorgio no longer responded. Then he heard the sounds of dinner.

Then the doors of the room closed. It was dark.

Then … a door opened. "Angeletta?" Giorgio whispered, lifting his head.

"No, it's me," Anselmo said in a low voice. "Listen, thief. Are you going to go on slandering me to my father?"

Suddenly Giorgio understood: several days before, he had seen Anselmo in the gang of the pockmarked boy. When Giorgio mentioned the matter later, Anselmo threatened revenge if Giorgio told on him.

"You think he's going to believe you? He has already gone to the police about you. Tomorrow they're coming to get you."

Anselmo stuck out his tongue and disappeared.

Police! Jail? Giorgio thought about how he would be led away. What if they heard about it back home? What would Nonna and Anita think? Nobody could get him out of this fix. Or might Alfredo …?

Giorgio felt along the wall behind the trash. Long ago, when he first came here, he had observed two loose boards. But after Angeletta got him to come to her in the evenings, he no longer thought about them. But now …

"Stop or I'll shoot." A hissed command. "What do you want?"

"I'm, I'm … I'm a chimneysweep. I just wanted to rest. Because …"

"Come along with me." With a firm grip the man pulled him through the bushes, down to the shore of the canal. A cluster of dark human shapes appeared to be squatting down there.

Giorgio was stood before them like a prisoner.

"What are you doing spying on us here? Go on, tell us. But no lies, understand?"

At the end of his story, Giorgio insisted once more that he was only looking for his friend Alfredo and that certainly he was no thief. At that, they all laughed.

"Whatever you say," the leader growled, "we're interested in what you can do. From now on, you're staying with us. Here, take something to eat—we know where there's food. Augusto, you tell him what he's got to do."

Giorgio hadn't eaten anything since early morning. He gladly took some food now. Above all, though, he wouldn't have dared to contradict anyone. From now on, he would be a thief after all.

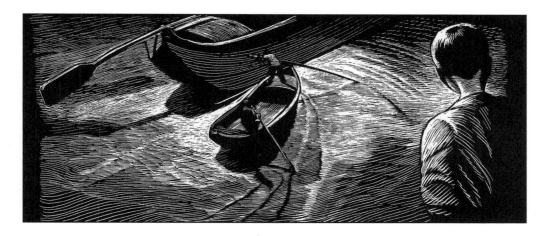

His job was to be the lookout. If someone was coming, he was supposed to meow.

"Understand?"

"But I'm no—"

"Quiet! Understand?"

"Yes."

From his post, Giorgio was able to see how the two men untied a boat and poled it toward a barge. You could hear hardly a splash. Everything passed in ghostly quiet. A little later, the two men returned to shore with their loot. The others helped them unload.

That was Giorgio's chance. Carefully he sneaked away and began to run.

Suddenly, from the shadow of an entrance, a policeman stepped in front of him.

Giorgio turned around and ran in the opposite direction—right into the arms of another policeman.

A whistle! More police arrived, and now they led Giorgio away.

Meanwhile, everything had changed for Angeletta too. There was one thought she just couldn't get out of her mind. A reflection in the mirror. Anselmo holding his father's purse. Everybody knew where Father's jacket always hung.

She had thought nothing of it. But now … Was this Anselmo's revenge? Giorgio had told her of the threat Anselmo had made. If only she could talk with Father. She became feverish with excitement. That was why Signora Rossi slept by her that night. And that was why Angeletta couldn't come to Giorgio.

Early in the morning, she was awakened by screaming.

Giorgio was gone. Mother raged! Angeletta called for her father. "Is it true that he's gone? Poor Giorgio."

"What," screeched Signora Rossi from the hall, "you're worried about that thief?"

"It wasn't him. It was that one." Angeletta pointed to her brother.

The father was ready to punish his son, but his mother protected him, and Anselmo crawled to hide in Giorgio's corner. By the time Master Rossi had taken the belt off its hook, the boy had escaped—out and away.

Signora Rossi once more breathed easy, but then she started to scream all over again. What would they tell the police when they came to fetch Giorgio? The master was able to calm her down. He didn't go to the police, he told her. Instead, he had gone to the Golden Pot that evening. And the innkeeper there had advised him to keep quiet about the whole affair.

Signora Rossi rehearsed a story that she would later be able to tell the neighbors. And the master took off to look for his chimneysweep boy. He inquired around in the taverns, but in the end, he did have to go to several police stations. At last, in the third one, they knew something about a boy who kept insisting that he was not a thief.

Home again, Giorgio realized the real battle was just beginning when Anselmo appeared and was forced to shake hands. Nonetheless, the master kept the promise he gave Giorgio on the way back. "You're not getting locked up again. As far as I'm concerned, after work you can go down to the courtyard."

It was only later that evening, when Angeletta told him all that had happened, that Giorgio realized how much he owed her.

Giorgio's days became more tolerable. He grew accustomed to the work and the master recognized his contribution. Still, the soot remained a torment, and his eyes and lungs suffered. But climbing up the chimney became easier and easier for Giorgio. The only thing he couldn't get used to was the taunting of the street boys.

"That's an old grudge," said Master Rossi. "Don't let it get to you."

But Giorgio couldn't help it. It was just too much. Even on holidays, the pockmarked boy lay in wait for him. He'd been tipped off by Anselmo.

Giorgio began to hunt for Alfredo. When he found him in the kitchen of the yellow-faced man, Giorgio was appalled at his appearance. Alfredo was even thinner than before, paler, and with feverish, hollow eyes like Angeletta's. It wasn't going well for Alfredo with his master, whom they secretly called The Lemon. Most of the time, he was drunk and gave Alfredo scarcely enough money to do their shopping. Indeed, Alfredo had to look after the whole household.

Alfredo's great hope lay in a brotherhood he had founded.

"Join us," he said, "and we'll protect you."

"But I'm in another part of town, and …"

"We're all over. And we're strong." Alfredo looked up to the clock on St. Babila. "If you want to come, we're going to gather in an hour."

On secret paths he went on ahead, toward an ancient wall. They crawled along the course of an old spring, feeling their way till they were standing in front of a door. Alfredo knocked.

From inside someone asked, "Password?"

"Ticino."

A bolt was slid back and they stepped inside. Baffled, Giorgio looked around.

"Who are you bringing there, Alfredo?"

"This is Giorgio."

"The one who was with you in Locarno?"

Giorgio recognized two boys from the boat. One of them, Antonio, told how they rescued themselves by swimming to the opposite shore.

"Quiet! Sit down!"

Giorgio was surprised. Alfredo hadn't said anything about being in charge here. Giorgio had no idea what was going to happen to him. First, the boys discussed accepting him. And because the one in charge wasn't allowed to vouch for the candidate, the two from Ticino acted as his sponsors. In fact, all the boys were from Ticino. Giorgio didn't become fully aware of that until he stood in front of Alfredo, who interrogated him formally.

"You're a Ticino chimneysweep boy?"

"Yes."

"You have to say 'Yes, boss,'" one of the witnesses whispered to him.

"Yes, boss."

After the interrogation came the swearing-in ceremony. Alfredo spoke in a solemn voice, and Giorgio repeated after him:

"… and promise for ever and ever to be a brave member of the gang of the Black Brotherhood, never to reveal their secrets or their cave, and to be true to every Brother. If I should break this vow, then …"

There followed a list of punishments, and then Giorgio had to repeat "I solemnly promise."

Alfredo regarded him seriously. Then he stepped forward and embraced Giorgio.

"That's not part of it," someone called out.

"He's my best friend. We swore loyalty to each other long ago."

Now they all jumped up, shook Giorgio's hand, and slapped him on the back.

Alfredo announced that they still had to discuss how to help the newcomer, and he explained some things. Giorgio hadn't been aware that the pockmarked boy was so notorious and that his gang even had a name. His "Wolves" were well known for the cowardly manner in which they sought out their battles. But now the Black Brothers hammered out a plan.

It was late when Giorgio secretly made his way to Angeletta. He was allowed to report about Alfredo, but not about his new friends, about the secret society, or that his own best friend was the founder and leader of it.

The next Sunday, Giorgio asked the master whether he could stay out longer. He wanted to go to the municipal park in the Public Gardens. But there was just one problem. Anselmo heard Giorgio's request and carried the news to the Wolves.

When Giorgio arrived at the big park, he saw his enemies right away. They were hiding behind trees or lurking in the shrubbery.

Giorgio pretended he was going for a walk without a care in the world. He looked around at the people and sauntered to a stone bench. "May I ask … is this seat taken?"

Then the first of the Wolves confronted him. "There you are! Now we've got you."

"You've got me, or have I got you?"

"Careful what you say. You're going to lose that smirk soon enough."

"What's all this?" growled the old man on the bench. "What do you want with him?"

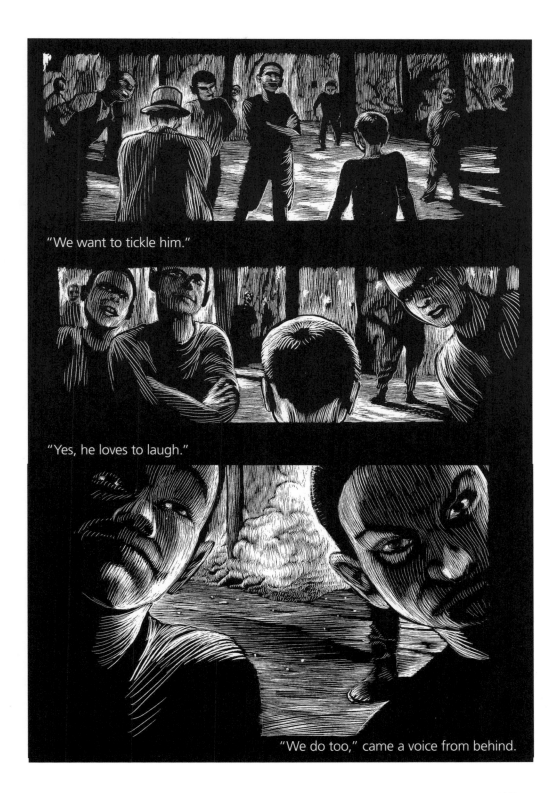

"We want to tickle him."

"Yes, he loves to laugh."

"We do too," came a voice from behind.

The Black Brothers charged in from every direction. Giorgio lunged at the pock-marked boy. The battle began.

"Sissies!" "Trash!" "Cowards!"

It did not last long. The Wolves ran away, the chimneysweep boys whistling and hooting after them. Suddenly the park police were on the scene.

The Black Brothers scattered in all directions.

"Good night, Giorgio," said Alfredo. "I'm tired. Don't you have to get out early tomorrow too?"

"Right, but … aren't you coming over? Angeletta wants to meet you."

They sneaked through the shed. Then Giorgio led the way. He looked about to see whether Master and Signora Rossi were asleep. And all seemed quiet with Anselmo.

Angeletta was delighted by their visit, and she asked with concern about their scrapes and wounds. No more excuses. The boys had to tell her.

Angeletta laughed dangerously loudly when she heard that Alfredo had beaten up her brother.

"That's why he came home so quietly. I hope he'll leave Giorgio in peace now."

Alfredo had almost fallen asleep. He said goodbye, and Giorgio led him downstairs. When he returned, Angeletta once more called to Giorgio to come in.

"Alfredo is not only tired. He's sick. Very sick," said Angeletta.

"I know. He's coughing."

"Not only that. His hands are feverish, like mine. The doctor said—"

"Angeletta?" Giorgio interrupted, frightened.

"I saw it right away when you two came in. He's hardly going to live any longer than I am. The doctor thinks …"

Giorgio had already begun to believe that everything would be better for him, here in Milan.

But when he realized that his best friend was suffering from a serious illness, he lay awake, sleepless, for a long time.

Angeletta was right. A week later, Antonio came, asking Giorgio to accompany him. Alfredo wanted to speak to him alone, said Antonio. So they went back together. Giorgio went upstairs to The Lemon's quarters. There, on a mattress on the floor, lay Alfredo, breathing heavily.

"Are you feeling bad?" Giorgio asked, somewhat embarrassed. He could feel how thin Alfredo's hand was— even bonier and hotter than Angeletta's.

Alfredo coughed harshly. Often he spat blood.

Alfredo began to reminisce, recalling the time he surprised Giorgio fishing.

For a moment both were silent. They thought about their homes.

Finally Alfredo said, "Back then we swore friendship and loyalty to each other."

What was he getting at? Alfredo needed to get a secret off his chest. Above all, Giorgio had to promise him that one day—when he was back in Ticino—he would visit Alfredo's sister, Bianca. Giorgio promised him that he would look after her.

The following evening Giorgio once again sneaked out to see his sick friend. When he heard The Lemon upstairs, he didn't dare go up. But later, when that drunkard had gone to the tavern, Alfredo was able tell Giorgio more of his story: how, as an orphan, he voluntarily signed himself up for Milan just so he could escape from his uncle. The uncle wanted to rob his sister and him of their inheritance. In fact, Alfredo was not at all poor. Quite the contrary.

Alfredo seemed relieved as he told Giorgio everything very precisely and gave him his instructions. "Till tomorrow, then."

"Yes, till tomorrow."

The next day Giorgio waited at the door. Alfredo was dead.

The Lemon wasn't going to bury him. From the time Alfredo got sick, The Lemon did nothing but drink as much as his money allowed. The chimneysweep boys realized right away that they could no longer keep the secret of their brotherhood. The most important task for them now was to see to it that their founder had a decent burial.

Finally, after many promises to the masters, the boys were able to get the morning off. With the little bit of money that they could scrape together, the Black Brothers bought a simple wooden casket.

"There are supposed to be two lilies on it," said Angeletta, handing Giorgio some money.

The Wolves got wind of the preparations for the burial, and early that very evening the two groups met again. So Giorgio was even more surprised that the pockmarked boy and his friends—even though they kept a distance—followed behind the coffin. Only Anselmo was distressed by this truce.

When Giorgio came home, Signora Rossi announced briskly, "No work, no soup."

The boy held his tongue. He didn't want to talk now. He crawled into his corner.

In Sonogno, winter meant snow and ice. The whole family was busy in the stable or the house. People sat together in the kitchen, whittling, braiding wicker, or weaving. They told stories and drank warm soup.

Here in Milan, winter was sometimes warm, sometimes cold; sometimes it was wet, sometimes dry. Even when he was sweating, Giorgio was freezing. Barefoot, always in the same clothes, and often with an empty stomach.

"Are you giving him enough to eat?" Master Rossi asked his wife. "He needs to be strong for the heavy work."

"Damn! Am I supposed to feed him till he's strong enough to kill us all? Wasn't that soup enough for him to beat up my Anselmo?"

In fact, Anselmo's backside was long healed from that last big fight. But Giorgio still had pains in his ribs. And the scar on his head kept breaking open when he banged it in a chimney.

At least Giorgio was able to be with Angeletta in the evening hours, and to stay connected to the Black Brothers. They wanted to make him Alfredo's successor. But he declined: "I live too far away from most of you. Choose Antonio."

The secret group then decided that both of them should be the leaders.

The master sensed that Giorgio was no longer the cheerful boy of times past.

"What's wrong with you?" he asked.

Sipping their schnapps to fend off the cold, the two sat in the tavern, protected from the wind that blew through the Via Manzoni.

"What's wrong with you?"

"I'm homesick."

"That'll pass, Giorgio."

Occasionally the master called him by his first name.

"Drink up. That drives away sorrows."

"And my chest hurts a lot."

"That's the soot. I used to have that too—at first."

"You?"

"Yes, I was a chimneysweep boy when I was ten. But luckily I signed up for only half a year."

"Then, didn't you … weren't you happy being a chimneysweep?"

"No, why, after all? Why should I be happy scrubbing furnaces?"

"But then why are you a chimneysweep at all?"

"Because … because my father and my grandfather … well, my father wanted the job to stay in the family and … I would rather have been a mason."

"Well then, go ahead and do that!" Giorgio said clearly.

"I never learned that trade. And I have a family, and they have to eat and … Come on, we've got to get to work. Put on a more cheerful face so that people won't say 'Here comes the merry Master Rossi with his sourpuss.' Understand?"

Giorgio pulled himself together. He shouted as loudly as he could. And he tried to shout merrily.

"It's dangerous in that heat. We've got to wait till the oven cools off."

"Impossible. We've got a lot of guests. The Signora has already begun complaining."

"Boy, you've got to get up there. Get your rag wet.—He's had lots of practice, he'll go all right."

The heat was unbearable. The wet rag over his mouth didn't help much.
Now, past the glowing hot iron, up into the heat.
A heat such as that time when …

A dry summer followed
the cold winter.
Nonna was complaining.
She knew what a June
without rain meant.
In the last drought
seven people
starved to death
in Sonogno.

Even his father complained that
in this heat, nothing could grow.
And in The Grotto
the men said that
the priest should go
through the village
with the saints of rain.
But the priest hesitated
when Roberto begged him to do it.
Finally he agreed after all.

Giorgio rang the bell as though
that would rescue the valley.

Men were carrying the tin coffin
bearing the saints of rain.
The procession circled around
the bell tower.
Giorgio rang and rang.
The priest called out,
"Oh bless us, oh bless us!"
And all joined in the chant:
"Oh bless us, oh bless us!"

When in the evening
there was still no rain,
when the next day
there was still no rain,
then Nonna said,
"This is a bad year.
It's going to end badly."

Giorgio could feel that he was stuck in
the chimney.
  He couldn't go up and he couldn't
go back.
  Something was holding him. He
was afraid.
  He heard the voice in the kitchen.
  "What's he doing all that time up
there?"
  "Fear not, he's a clever boy."
  He was unable to answer.
  "Hello! What's going on with
you?"
  When on the third call Giorgio still
did not respond, the master tried to
grasp his legs. Bricks fell down … and
then, all of a sudden—
  "Watch out!" a maid screamed.
  "Is he dead?"

"Signora," said the cook with a flat
voice. "Signora, we've got a dead one ..."

"What?" The lady of the house stepped up
to the table. "My God, who is that?"

"You had been complaining about the smoke. So
we found the chimneysweep and ..."

"Did you get a doctor yet ...? No, forget about that! Doctor
Casella is one of the guests:"

"Yes, right here," said someone in the doorway. "What happened?"

The doctor gave Giorgio respiration until he opened his eyes. Then he bound the wound on Giorgio's head and ordered Master Rossi to let the weakened boy rest for a few days. "It's a serious business. I've never in my life seen such a starved boy in Milan."

The master understood. He was himself deeply frightened when Giorgio fell out of the chimney as though he were dead.

But Signora Rossi didn't want to hear anything about it. She argued with her husband when he came home late, holding up the weakened boy. She refused to help in any way, and only grudgingly let her husband do anything for the boy. And the next morning her screaming got even worse. Master Rossi had suggested that Anselmo help him for a few days.

In the end, the master went off alone. When he came back in the evening, worn out and with little accomplished, there was a carriage standing in the courtyard.

"That's for you," hissed the carpenter who lived there too.

Master Rossi recognized the doctor and made a sort of bow.

On the stairs, there was whispered gossip.

"Did Angeletta take a turn for the worse?"

"No, the doctor asked about a boy."

"Anselmo?"

"No, I saw him in the market today."

"Listen, listen. I think it was about the chimneysweep boy."

"What! A doctor for that rascal?"

Doctor Casella sat down next to Giorgio.

"Where are you from?"

"The Verzasca Valley."

"Then you're from Ticino."

Giorgio nodded.

"Me too. I'm from Lugano."

"Alfredo is also from—Alfredo was also from …"

Giorgio turned silent. He looked around to see whether anyone was listening, and then he began to tell: about Alfredo, about the Black Brotherhood. When he was finished, Doctor Casella patted his head and called for the Rossis. Signora Rossi arrived first, gesticulating wildly as the doctor recommended that Giorgio take some days of rest. Giorgio didn't have merely an infection from smoke inhalation. His lungs had also been affected—and, worst of all: "The boy is starving."

"That's not true. Every day I give him …"

"You can talk all you want. I can see it clearly. But tell me, Master Rossi, how much do you earn per day?"

"Five to six. If I'm alone, three, and with—"

"What! Don't lie," Signora Rossi interrupted. "Doctor, he brings home eight lire; last week, nine, in fact. And the boy has to watch out that this drunk doesn't spend all his money in the tavern."

"Fine. I'll pay you five lire for each day the boy rests. Ten now, and ten more when I see that you stick to the agreement. The boy should …"

"He's going to have it so good, he'll think he's in heaven," said Signora Rossi, sweet as sugar.

And as the doctor reached for his pocket, she added, "Shouldn't he be lying in our daughter's room?"

"Who is that?" asked Angeletta as her mother and the stranger carried in a mattress.

"A doctor," said Giorgio, almost proudly. "He brought me back to life. He's from Lugano, from Ticino."

For a moment Doctor Casella spoke with Angeletta. Then he himself fixed Giorgio's bed, and he sent Signora Rossi to the apothecary and to the butcher.

"So—now we'll not be interrupted. Giorgio, please tell me how you came to Milan. Start at the beginning."

When Signora Rossi returned, Doctor Casella gave her precise instructions for the medicine. The powder was to be for Angeletta; the drops were for Giorgio. And then he examined the meat purchases.

"That's for both of them. Make a strong soup, with vegetables and butter."

"Nobody has ever gone hungry in my house," said Signora Rossi.

"Well, up till today, the boy doesn't seem to have had much meat or bouillon."

"Are you starting that again?" Master Rossi's wife stood there, hands on her hips.

"No." Doctor Casella laughed. "I hear you, and I'm leaving. But ..." He turned around once more. "Just to make sure, I'm having food brought over from the hotel. Giorgio has my address."

It was like paradise on earth. Never before had Giorgio lain on a real mattress. And then for breakfast there was coffee with milk in it and white bread, too, at noon delicacies Giorgio had never dreamed of from the hotel kitchen, and in the evening a hearty meat soup.

Angeletta was happy to have company. Over and over, Giorgio had to tell her his stories. In return she would read to him from a thick book. Doctor Casella was astonished that Giorgio couldn't read and had never been to school.

Four days later, when Giorgio was passing through the hallway, Signora Rossi looked at him bitterly. Doctor Casella had asked that the boy come to the city.

In front of the hotel City of Rome stood a man in uniform. He confronted Giorgio.

"Scat! Get out of here."

"But I have to go see Doctor Casella. He's waiting for me."

"Then let him wait, and away with you! You're scaring away the guests."

But when Giorgio pulled the doctor's calling card out of his pocket, the man beckoned to a bellboy and sent him in with the card.

Very soon the doctor was standing before Giorgio. "So, what shall we do?"

"I'm thinking you want to show me the market."

"I suggest we'd better go into the galleria, where the stores are."

They stepped into a shoe store—but not for wooden shoes. This store sold leather shoes of all sorts, shoes for ladies and gentlemen.

"Which ones do you want?" Doctor Casella enjoyed Giorgio's amazement.

"Me? In Sonogno I went around barefoot."

Even trying on clothes was an entirely new experience for Giorgio. But after he had acquired trousers, shirts, a jacket, a belt, and even a cap and a muffler, Giorgio wanted to look at himself.

There, in the mirror window of the hairdresser, he contemplated his image. Dressed like a gentleman!

"What do you think of yourself?"

"I don't know … I … how can I thank you?"

"I'm happy that you're better. That's something that has to be celebrated."

Later, when they were sitting in a restaurant, Doctor Casella suddenly said, "Tomorrow I'm driving back to Lugano."

"But—you wanted to come see the Black Brothers."

"Yes, I did promise that. Are you going to meet this evening?"

When they met again later, Giorgio arrived in his old clothes. He had carefully packed away the new ones and hidden them in the shed. The only thing he had brought into the house was Doctor Casella's present for Angeletta.

Now, in the street behind St. Babila, Giorgio was worried whether the doctor would manage to crawl through those narrow openings and tunnels. But even though it was slow going, it did work. They were at the door now, and they knocked.

"Password?" a voice asked.

"Ticino."

Giorgio was given a hearty welcome. His friends had missed him. When finally Doctor Casella straightened up and stepped into the light, all the boys were silent for a moment. And then they all spoke at once.

"Quiet!" said Giorgio firmly. "I'll explain everything to you."

He recounted how this man had saved his life, how he had looked after his well-being, and how he helped him get back a little of his freedom from Signora Rossi.

"Yes," said the doctor. "I've heard incredible stories about your lives, and I want to learn more about them. That's why I am here today."

One after the other, the boys now told about their fates: orphans ill used by their foster parents; children sold by their parents because of poverty. Certainly none of them was there of his own accord.

Occasionally Doctor Casella raised the lamp higher in order to better see a boy. Their emaciated bodies, scarcely covered by their rags, told the story of their daily lives and exploitation. When the doctor asked about their sleeping arrangements and their food, one of them laughed, saying, "We're not allowed to get fat or we'd get stuck in the chimneys."

"Listen," said Doctor Casella after he had taken notes on their stories. "Your parents—or whoever—have made contracts. That complicates matters. But what I can do is to write about you. I'll turn to the Swiss consul in Milan and I'll report on your lives in the Swiss newspapers. In Ticino. Here, I'm really not able to help you."

He laid his hand on Antonio's shoulder. "Do you have a cash box? There—buy yourselves warm stockings and see to it that you survive the winter well. I'll see you again, in Lugano. Giorgio knows my address. Till then."

"Why can you help only in Lugano?" Giorgio asked as he was leading Doctor Casella into the alley again. "How did you mean that?"

"Just like I said."

"We're supposed to …" Giorgio hesitated for a moment. "Are we supposed to run away?"

"I didn't say that. Do you understand? All the best to you."

"You too. Goodbye—and thank you!"

Giorgio returned to his friends, who were just then dividing up the money. Each one got a lira. The rest they put aside. It was intended for those who really were going to escape.

Then he ran home as quickly as he could. He knew that he was still weak, but he looked forward to unpacking his new things. But … the package had disappeared!

Giorgio asked Angeletta. She knew nothing about it. And when he wanted to lie down, he discovered that his mattress had been taken out of the room.

"Mother said you've got to sleep over there again."

Suddenly all Giorgio's courage drained from him. He crawled off into his corner.

"Get up!" Signora Rossi woke Giorgio with a kick. Then, as he looked around him, she demanded to know what he was looking for.

"My new clothes. The doctor gave them all to me. Real shoes, even. And to top it all off, a belt, a cap, and a muffler."

"Sure, and a coat, a vest, an umbrella," the missus scoffed. "Are you going to say that I took your things away?"

The master came into the kitchen. He had no idea what to believe and was simply eager to get to work.

By noon the package still hadn't appeared. Giorgio once more had to eat in the chimney corner. Soup. Nothing else.

There—from the hallway suddenly came the sound of footsteps, a sort of military tread.

Anselmo strutted in.

"My shoes!" Even Giorgio was frightened by his own outburst.

"What?" yelled Signora Rossi.

"Yes." Giorgio gathered all his courage. "He's wearing my shoes."

Anselmo acted unconcerned. He spooned up his soup, saying that in the morning he had been at the market with his mother.

Because Giorgio refused to drop the topic, Signora Rossi screamed at him again, "You're trying to say I took your clothes!"

"Yes, and …"

By now the woman was in a rage. She beat on Giorgio till her husband restrained her.

Very quietly Giorgio said once again, "Those are my shoes."

"Meathead!" The master joined in the shouting.

"There are a thousand shoes like that in Milan. How are you going to prove that …"

"I'll go get the doctor." Giorgio jumped up, ran into the hallway and—suddenly he stood stock still.

"He left. This very morning."

As recently as the day before, Giorgio had wanted to remain with Master Rossi and Angeletta.

Today, he knew that he would run away. When Master Rossi lay down for his midday nap and his wife and Anselmo remained in the kitchen, Giorgio went very quickly to see Angeletta. Then he disappeared.

All afternoon he sat in the cavern of the Black Brotherhood.

Odd noises floated into the darkness. Time passed slowly.

At last, the first friends appeared. They were amazed to find Giorgio there. Others came in later. They reported that already Giorgio was being hunted.

Nonetheless, he once more that night sneaked back to Angeletta.

He had promised her. Through the shed and up through the loose boards he worked his way into the house.

"Take this," said Angeletta. "A remembrance of me."

She sat up in bed, undid the little chain with a gold cross, and hung it about Giorgio's neck.

"The gold cross? The one from your aunt?"

"Yes, wear it. I don't like to think back to her. But you are to remember me. Will you tell your Anita about me?"

When Angeletta extricated herself from his embrace, she asked once more, "How will I know that you've arrived?"

"There are three or four of us who are running away together. We'll stay in touch with those we leave behind. Farewell."

When Giorgio returned to his corner, he heard somebody in the kitchen. Anselmo had been expecting that Giorgio would return. But he had fallen asleep during his wait. Now he called for help.

Giorgio heard footsteps, and as he tried to slip away through the loose boards, someone gripped his legs. Giorgio kicked out at him and escaped.

But outside in the courtyard, too, he heard people coming down the stairs.

For Dante, the youngest in the group, things didn't go any better. His master had sent dogs in pursuit of him. But the Wolves—those other boys—rescued him. Because his leg was bleeding, they carried him to their hideaway. The Black Brothers were glad for this help. But they were fearful, too, lest now more people would know about their secret cave.

Then, in the night, four Black Brothers sneaked along the canal, out of the city. Antonio, Augusto, Dante, and Giorgio.

The December morning was clear and cold. Even from a distance, the four could see several people standing around the customs station. People with dogs. Police?

"Somebody betrayed us," murmured Dante, hobbling along behind.

"Not necessarily," said Antonio. "If they're looking for us, then they'd be searching on the path northward. So let's get going."

"The man with the scar." Giorgio almost shouted out loud. "And next to him …"

"Anselmo! That's Anselmo!" The boys threw themselves into the bushes between the street and the canal. They wanted to turn back, go back to the last bridge.

They met a fisherman who took them to the far shore.

Now they were able to avoid villages and resume their way toward the mountains.

One time Augusto went alone up to a house to ask directions.

A man cordially showed him the way. But when the man saw that Augusto had all those other boys with him, his suspicions were aroused.

Had the police already been here, asking about four runaways?

Suddenly they heard human voices and dogs barking.

"Over there!" shouted Antonio. "Here they come! Quick, into the woods!"

"No, that's no good for us. Better over the other way, to those barns ..."

"Yes! The forest behind them is more dense too." Without Dante, they'd be faster. But when other dogs started barking in the farmyard, the police dogs stopped their chase.

When their pursuers had gone, the boys waited a little longer in their hiding place.

Then they stood up. They wanted to keep going toward the mountains.

The night in a haystack didn't do much to refresh them. Dante's wound was bleeding again and every barking dog made them start up with alarm.

They rose and got on the road before the sun dissipated the fog.

If only they could have asked somebody how far it still was to the border.

When they saw a farmer who had just loaded hay onto his wagon, they did not hesitate. They ran toward him.

Giorgio hoped the farmer would help them and not turn them over to the police.

"Hide you on the wagon? Why?"

Antonio started to tell about their misery in Milan. Giorgio interrupted him. "My father is a farmer too."

"Well, so? What good is that going to do if they catch me helping you? Am I supposed to hang for you boys?"

"Dogs! You hear them?" Augusto pointed to the poplar woods.

Giorgio reached into his jacket. "Here. I'll give you this, but help us—please."

The farmer looked at Giorgio's gold cross with curiosity. "Stolen?"

"No, a present for remembrance. Please help us."

"Okay," the man muttered. "Hop up there, crawl in."

"Get those mongrels of yours back or I'll … I've got my whip here."

"Calm down! Those dogs won't hurt you."

"But my oxen. What do you want anyway? What's this all about?"

The second policeman arrived and started to explain.

The man with the scar continued his scolding, jabbing angrily at the hay.

The boys squeezed themselves smaller. They could smell the liquor on him.

They wanted to crawl toward the center, but on the other hand, they weren't supposed to move at all.

Then the farmer asked about the reward.

"Twenty-five thousand. The chimneysweep boys' masters have promised that."

The farmer appeared to be impressed. "Those must really be rascals then."

Giorgio bit his sleeve. Dante wanted to scream.

"So, there's four of them, you're looking for four. One of them limps." The farmer sat high on his cartload and now he spoke very quietly. "I sent them over there. They asked how to get through the swamp. I advised them it would be better to go to Varese. Now, how much do I get?"

The man with the scar shook his fist at him. The police let the dogs run and took off across the field.

When the farmer came to a stop in his own yard, laughingly he called out, "All passengers, get off!"

Toward evening, the farmer's son came home from the village. Even as he was stepping into the doorway, he reported that the police were looking for thieves. He was startled by the boys, and even more so when he heard their story. No older than himself, and already in flight!

They all sat down to supper. The soup was not only hot but nourishing as well, and there was bread to go along with it. While the farmer's wife tended to Dante's wounds and bandaged them, the boys discussed what to do next.

Shortly after midnight, the farmer's son fetched the four friends out of the hay where they had been resting. In the kitchen they were treated to milk. Then the farmer's wife gave them a loaf of bread to eat along the road. And then they left, walking in single file. The farmer's son led the way. He was familiar with the secret paths, the smugglers' trails.

It had been daylight for some time when they first saw the shimmering lake between the trees.

"Lake Lugano. And over there, that's Switzerland."

From a hiding place they surveyed their position. Then they made for one of the boats. But hardly had they pushed off from the shore than they saw two boats coming from Porto Ceresio.

"Stop!" someone shouted. "Stop! Police."

Wasn't that the man with the scar over there in the boat? Somebody fired into the air.

Augusto pulled up a board from the flooring to help with the rowing. But the pursers were gaining on them. "Faster!" cried Dante, who wasn't rowing. "Faster."

Then, intently, he peered ahead. "Look, over there, the fog ..."

Tollmaster Riva was used to the west wind bringing all sorts of things to the spit of land called Morcote. But a boat with children? Four sleeping children? They started up when he leaned over them. But as soon as they understood that they were on the Swiss side the boys laughed and cried. Riva, aware that search boats had come out from the other side the day before, refused to show the boys the right path. Had he shown them, he'd know where they could be tracked down, and that was something he didn't want to know. He simply let the boys run off.

Without stopping, without eating, the boys headed northward along the shoreline road. When they came to the first houses of Lugano, they asked for Doctor Casella.

"Up there, on the hill. You can't miss it."

The house was even more magnificent than they had imagined. A villa.

The doctor wasn't home, but one of the boys squeezed past the maid.

"Is one of you Giorgio?" she inquired.

Toward evening, Doctor Casella came home. He was surprised by how quickly the boys had followed his suggestion. He insisted that he had not actually advised them to flee. The next day, when they were in Lugano, Giorgio understood.

Giorgio waited by Casella's carriage while the doctor visited a patient. Then, suddenly, on the other side of the street, he saw the man with the scar. Giorgio hid behind the horse. But the man wouldn't have recognized him in any case. Gloomily looking straight ahead, he disappeared into a tavern.

Just as soon as Giorgio had told the doctor all this, the doctor took him to the police station.

"Doctor, is that you? What can I do for you, sir?"

The doctor said nothing about Milan, nothing about the boys. He merely asked the policeman whether he still recalled the boat accident.

Quickly the commandant summoned two policemen. When the three entered the tavern, the man with the scar insisted that he was not the wanted Antonio Luini. And when they called in Giorgio, the man was doubly insistent. "That's the thief! He stole from his master," said the man with the scar. "He broke the contract and he's the one you've got to arrest. Not me!"

Antonio Luini was actually sought by the police only because of his role in the accident at sea.

Months later, Doctor Casella recalled the judgment the court had reached in the case of the man with the scar: "Five years in jail. And after that, exile."

Nine years passed. It was spring in the meadows, and the apple and the pear trees were in bloom. Narcissi blossomed along the riverbank. And on this April morning, a young man and a woman—the young man's wife—could be seen riding on the narrow path from Bellinzona to Locarno.

"This is where we've got to turn, I think," the young man said.

"Why don't you ask," urged his wife.

"No—no mistaking it," he said. "This river is the Verzasca … and that's the path up there."

They ascended ever more steeply along the cliff edge.

After a time, they looked down across the plain. The mountaintops were covered with snow, and far to the right their summits were mirrored in the blue waters of Lago Maggiore.

The two continued on their truly dangerous path until they came to Brione.

"Where are you headed?" asked the innkeeper after he had brought them a small round of cheese.

"Sonogno," said the young man.

"Did you lose something there?" joked the host.

"I'm the new teacher," the young man replied.

"Well … what'll it be next!" the host exclaimed. "Next thing you know, they'll be wanting to build a road there!"

Again the two got under way, walking their horses until they came to a little stream.

"Here, this is where I first saw the man with the scar, and knew he had come to buy me," said Giorgio. "I wanted to roll a boulder down on him," he continued. After a pause he added, "But somehow I must have sensed that this man with the scar was my fate, and that I would have to go to Milan in order to find you, Bianca."

As the two approached Sonogno, Giorgio insisted that they first ride to the inn, to The Grotto. The old innkeeper was still there.

"The new teacher! That's great," he exclaimed. "The school is almost finished. And they've been working on fixing up your lodging all year." And then he blinked.

"Giorgio," he exclaimed. He hardly trusted his eyes.

Giorgio, for his part, wanted to know all about his parents. Were they well? Was Nonna still alive? And the twins? They were working in Locarno, he learned.

But there was news indeed. Giorgio now had two little sisters and a brother, six, seven, and eight years old—born, of course, after he had left.

And when, later, Bianca and Giorgio came to the house, the parents and Nonna, now very thin, very frail, welcomed the young couple, having no idea who they were.

They talked amiably.

"How many children do you have?" asked Giorgio.

"Three—these three here." Giorgio's mother pointed to the little ones.

"Three?" Giorgio asked. "I heard that you had six."

"Did have, once upon a time …" The father busily stuffed his pipe. "Two have left to make their way in the world, and one died," he muttered.

"Oh, why did you ever sell him," Giorgio's mother moaned. "I'd rather you had let me die."

"If he's dead, he's in heaven. And if he's alive, as Nonna says, then he'll have forgiven us by now."

"You really think he's dead?" asked Giorgio. "What if I were to tell you he's alive?"

"You think … you really think …?" His mother gasped.

"Yes," said Giorgio, "he's alive."

His mother approached him. "Oh … oh!" she exclaimed. She threw herself on him.

His father, too, embraced him now. And the two little girls swung on Giorgio's arms and legs. And little Emilio stared at his new brother, wide-eyed.

"And me, aren't you going to hug me?" asked old Nonna.

He embraced her gently. "No, no, hug me tight," she said. "Squeeze me to death if you like." And so he hugged her again.

"Well then," Nonna said. "Wasn't it right that I told you to go away back then?" she asked, shaking Giorgio with her thin arms. "Go, I said, go if you're a real man. Go, see the world. And now, introduce me to your wife, won't you."

Bianca came forward from the chimney corner, where she had been taking it all in.

"A fine woman you seem to be," said Nonna. "And do you love your husband?"

Bianca nodded. "With all my heart!" she said.

"How did it happen that you became a teacher?" asked his father.

"That's a long story, and I'm going to save it for another day," said Giorgio.

And Nonna, having gone back to her corner, chuckled to herself. "I always knew that he'd come back—and that the boy would really make something of himself."